Swallow the Leader

A COUNTING BOOK

by DANNA SMITH

Illustrated by
KEVIN SHERRY

CLARION BOOKS
Houghton Mifflin Harcourt
Boston   New York

Clarion Books
3 Park Avenue
New York, New York 10016

Text copyright © 2016 by Danna Smith
Illustrations copyright © 2016 by Kevin Sherry

Clarion Books is an imprint of
Houghton Mifflin Harcourt Publishing Company.
www.hmhco.com
The illustrations in this book were created in layers using watercolor
backgrounds, paper cutouts, and paint on acetate sheets.
The text was set in Aunt Mildred.

Library of Congress Cataloging-in-Publication Data is avaialble.
LCCN 2015034865

Manufactured in China
SCP 10 9 8 7 6 5 4 3 2 1
4500596987

For Kayden, Koel, Maddix, Mason, Bellamie, Brier, Keylin, Camden, and Kace.
And with a special thank you to my amazing agent, Ronnie Ann Herman. —D.S.

Dedicated to the legendary Devlin Rice. —K.S.

1 Fish

2 Fish

Follow the leader.
Do as I do.
Splash when I'm splashing,
then I'll follow you.

3 Fish

Follow the leader
to coral caves.
Snap like a crab.
Ride on the waves.

4 **Fish**

Follow the leader.
Waggle your tail.
Swim to the surface.
Blow like a whale.

5 Fish

Follow the leader.
Play like I play.
Pretend you are me.
Flap like a ray.

6 Fish

Follow the leader
to the lagoon.
Puff like a blowfish,
round as the moon.

7 Fish

Follow the leader
into the dark.
Hush when I'm quiet.
Hide from a shark.

8 Fish

Follow the leader.
Go where I go.
Trot like a seahorse.
Stop when I whoa.

9 Fish

Follow the leader.
Leap when I leap.
Hurdle a turtle,
down in the deep.

10 Fish

Follow the leader.
Float on your back.
Open your mouth and . . .

. . . eat a sea snack.

Gulp!

Uh-oh!

Swallow the leader . . .

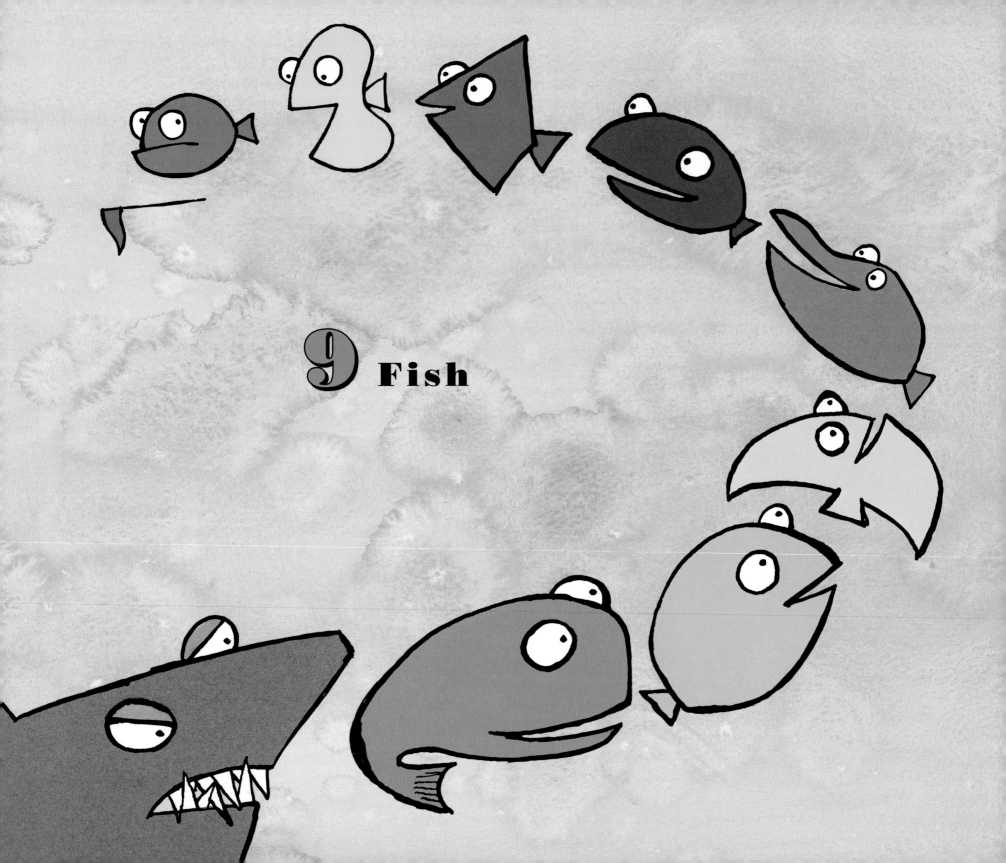

9 Fish

8 Fish

7 Fish

6 Fish

5 Fish

4 Fish

3 Fish

2 Fish

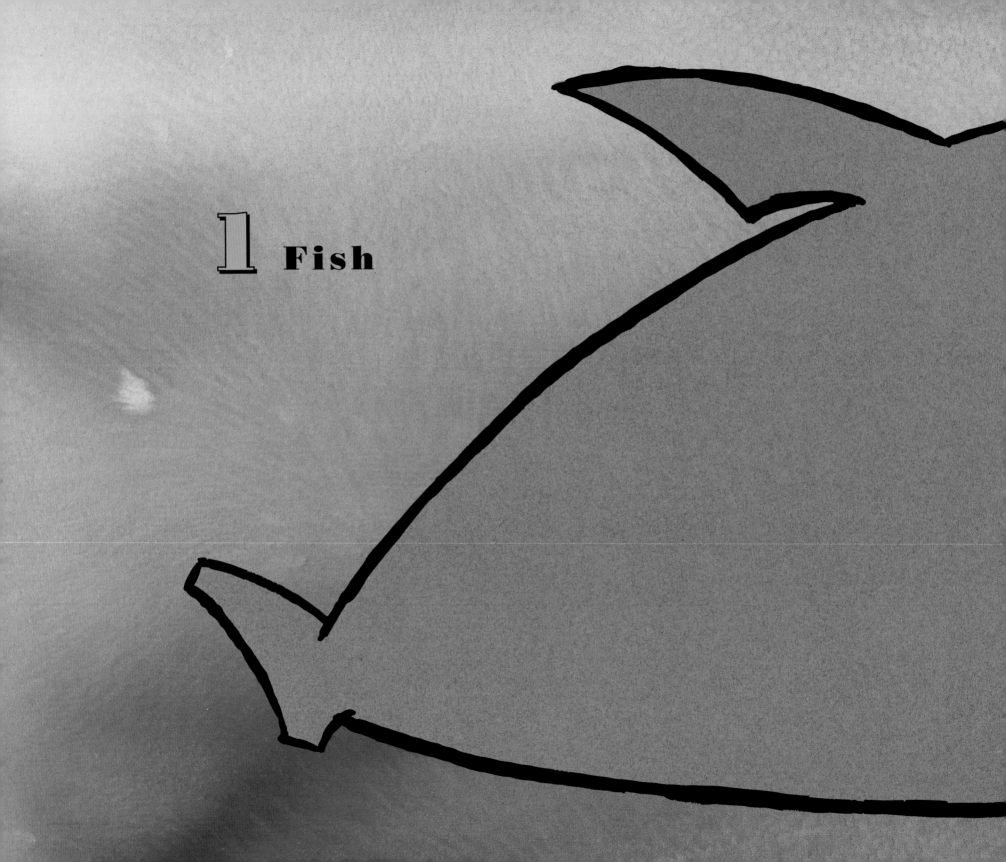

1 Fish

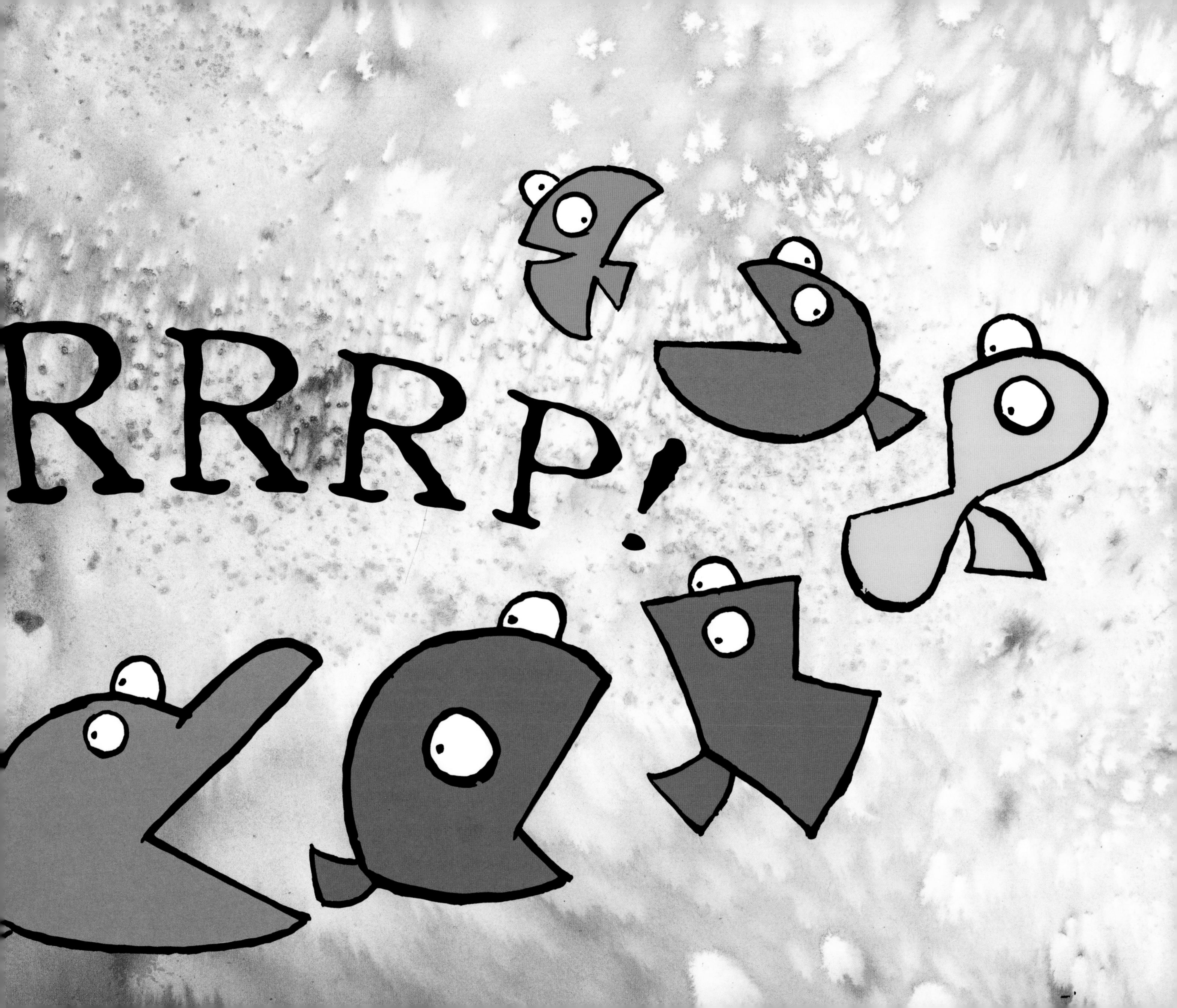
RRRP!

10 Fish

Follow the leader.
Do as I do.
You followed me;
now I'll follow you.